FOREWORD

Young Writers is proud to present, 'Welcome to Wonderland – Western England'.

For our latest mini saga competition, we asked secondary school pupils to create a story with a beginning, middle and end, with the added challenge of keeping to 100 words.

The result is this collection of fantastic fiction where our writers invite you in to their whole new worlds. Get ready for an adventure as you discover different dimensions with war and battles, sweet dream lands, disturbing dystopias and never-ending nightmares. From the weird to the wonderful, there is something here to suit everyone.

There was a great response to this competition and the standard of entries was excellent, so I'd like to say a big thank you and well done to everyone who entered.

Zak Flint

CONTENTS

Abbots Bromley School, Rugeley

Courtney Geer (11) 1
Georgina Campbell (12) 2

Abbotsholme School, Uttoxeter

Philippa Oldacre (14) 3

Adcote School For Girls, Shrewsbury

Rhiannon Elizabeth 4
Williams (13)
Freya May Owen (12) 5
Lucy Johnson (13) 6
Alex Hughes (13) 7
Rebecca Collins (13) 8

Aldersley High School, Wolverhampton

Caine Edmund Cawley (13) 9
Kyle Onyx Skett (11) 10
Jake Aldersley (11) 11
Matthew Baker (12) 12
Bradley David Newman (11) 13
Sean Reeves (11) 14
Sophie Blakeway (11) 15
Leon Flynn (11) 16
Zilan Abdulla (11) 17
Anni Clarke-Shannon 18
Jacob Smith (12) 19
Cianan Duncombe (11) 20
Alexander Gilpin (11) 21
Aro Hassan (11) 22
Vina Mahmood (12) 23

Owen Aulton (11) 24
Damian-Jake Fisher (11) 25
Kieron John Cawley (11) 26
Sam Quinton (12) 27
Jamie Pilsbury (11) 28
Siobhan Dorrance (12) 29
Kyle James Logan (11) 30
Darya Kakai (11) 31
Gracie-Rae Osborn (11) 32
Leah Ariel McInnis (11) 33
Leroy Uche (13) 34
Oumou Kesso Barry (12) 35
Priya Kaur Rayet (11) 36
Matthew Bickerton (11) 37
Niamh Clarke-Shannon (12) 38
Jamie Passmore (11) 39
Tyler John David Preece (15) 40
Samuel Nestor (11) 41
Gabriella Farrier (8) 42
Holly Lane (12) 43
Paige Susan Noble (11) 44
Nikola Armale (11) 45
Mathew Wynne Jones (11) 46
Eniola Raheem (13) 47
Ben Walker (11) 48
Amanda Ward (11) 49
Fletcher Rushbury (12) 50

Bishop Vesey's Grammar School, Sutton Coldfield

Noah Green (12) 51
Charles Michael Fortescue 52
Hubbard (12)
Thomas Cartmill (11) 53
Mackenzie Davis (13) 54

Joshua Tranchant (12)	55
Ishan Mitra	56
Matthew Merrill (11)	57
Thomas James Green (12)	58
Ethan Finney (12)	59
Vraj Tushar Shah (13)	60
James Foxall (12)	61
Oliver Henry Gray-Nimmo (13)	62
Leon Lwanga	63

Concord College, Shrewsbury

Yehia Shawkat (13)	64
Penri William Edward Jones (13)	65
Eden Skye Broadbent (13)	66
Rose Smith (13)	67
Olivia Marcham (13)	68
T'Oluwafe Eyifewa Onadele (13)	69
Thomas Dix (14)	70

Fairfield High School, Hereford

Arthur Dimbylow (12)	71
Kate Jessica Coupland (12)	72
Adam Smith (12)	73
Holly Prior (12)	74
Beth Llewellin (12)	75
Maisie White (12)	76
Lucas Marchant (13)	77
Ella Gibbs (13)	78
Christiana Mills (13)	79
Bridget Elizabeth Morgan (12)	80
Daniel Smith (13)	81
Lewis Lloyd (13)	82
Alexis Skye Powell (13)	83
Rudi Ambrose Davies (12)	84
Dewi Meredith	85
Aaron Pearson (13)	86
Evie White (12)	87
Lucy Baker (13)	88
Jasmine Jefferson (13)	89
Fred Davies (12)	90
Faith Roberts (12)	91

Madeley Academy, Telford

Ellie Tyler (13)	92
Joshua James Allen (13)	93
Dylan Harris (12)	94
Ethan Green (12)	95
Courtney Jade Edgar (13)	96
Jamie George Morris (13)	97
Isabelle Edney (13)	98
Caitlyn Webb (12)	99
Warren Whittaker (12)	100
Isabel Black (11)	101

Shrewsbury Academy, Shrewsbury

Dylan Livingston (13)	102
Lucia Malvone (13)	103

The Aconbury Centre, Hereford

Kyle Williams (12)	104
Kieron Clements (12)	105

The Burton Borough School, Newport

Mark Dixon (14)	106
Jessica Broome (12)	107
Jacob Johnson (14)	108

The Kingsley School For Girls, Leamington Spa

Emily Bell (11)	109
Sylvia Sinclair (11)	110
Izzie Gore (12)	111
Chantal Soiné (14)	112
Amber Venn	113
Matilda Milner (12)	114
Laura Jane Silk (13)	115
Katie Jones (13)	116
Phoebe Turner (11)	117
Katie Walsh (14)	118
Ishika Doug (11)	119

Lily Lawson (13) 120
Beth Rickett (13) 121
Abi Lawson (11) 122
Grace Green (12) 123
Isabella Larucci 124
Kitty Lawson (11) 125
Grace Heather Shipley (14) 126
Olivia Marshall (11) 127
Amy Barrett (11) 128
Jessica Bennett 129
Georgie Green (14) 130
Charlotte Lucy Green (11) 131
Mia Featherstone (11) 132
Sophie Elizabeth Maguire (13) 133
Morgan Anne Marie Bethell (12) 134
Pia Brougham (13) 135
Maddie Mia McClean (13) 136
Grace Smith (14) 137
Maya Illingworth (11) 138
Eliza Chamberlain-Sparks (11) 139

Tuition, Medical & Behaviour Support Service, Bridgnorth

Will James Coadey (13) 140
Leo Kane (14) 141
Elliot Jones (14) 142

West Midlands Construction UTC, Wolverhampton

Emily Cross (14) 143
Georgina Tranter-Wilkes (15) 144
Gurpal Singh Sahota (14) 145
Danielle Lace Bowdler-Silvester (15) 146
Jai Ghai (14) 147
Gurkeitan Singh Barring (14) 148

THE MINI SAGAS

Alien Invasion!

Bustling streets, packed town, crowded country, overflowing world! This is today, but what about tomorrow? Aliens found and discovered planets we've never even heard of! Will it be a nice, caring world? No! We currently live upside down, turned around! If only we weren't so mad about technology! Jackie Johnson predicts that aliens will take over the world we call Earth, but when will that day be? Any day, hour or minute! Better get packing soon. Off to another planet we go; maybe Mars or Jupiter. You don't want to be there when *they* arrive!

Courtney Geer (11)
Abbots Bromley School, Rugeley

The Quarrel

You could hear the sounds of guns going off and the voices of the army commanders giving orders. We were in no-man's-land. It all started with a little quarrel between Ariana and Erin, and then it escalated into a war! From there, the trenches grew, the friendships broke and so did the trust. It was two against eight. We did not have long to end this, and it was not going to end well. The flags were raised; the first gunshot had been fired. This was happening: the war of year seven!

Georgina Campbell (12)
Abbots Bromley School, Rugeley

Too Late

Pippania cast the spell onto the forest of evil and stone began to spread upon the horrors that lay within. 'What now?' said Anastasia.

'Give the spell time to work,' said Pippania. As the fairies tried to fly away and leave the evil forces behind, the wind suddenly changed and blew them back into the forest. With hearts racing and wings fluttering, they thumped to the now stone ground of the forest. Before they could rise, the spell turned upon them. Anastasia screamed, but it was too late, and they lay stuck in their own spell, for all eternity.

Philippa Oldacre (14)
Abbotsholme School, Uttoxeter

Before And Beneath

Luminous spirals, iridescent and undulating, rise from the depths. Translucent domes drift past myriad discs of rotating light. A creature, soft and thoughtful, glides through its kaleidoscope world with sinuous grace, amid spectrums of endless colour. Other beings brush past it fluidly; contact is rapid and intelligent. The creature moves on. Suddenly, a past echo, a distant tether, compels the creature to ascend. Rising through vast and ancient waters, it breaks the surface.

All is infinite sea, limitless sky. The world speaks of something lost. The creature knows. Visions stir; deserts, mountains and savannahs unfold. 'Earth. Once there was Earth.'

Rhiannon Elizabeth Williams (13)
Adcote School For Girls, Shrewsbury

Loch Love

Andy Blackwell always loved beautiful Scotland, with its large lochs. It was a place where he felt happy. His friends saw him as a weak writer. Once, he jumped into a loch and saved a woman. That was the sort of man he was.

Andy walked to the window, reflecting on his surroundings. Rain hammered like galloping horses. Then he saw something in the distance, or rather someone. It was the figure of Millie. She was charming. Andy gulped. He stepped outside as Millie approached.

She said, 'I love you.'

'I feel the same,' said Andy with a grin.

Freya May Owen (12)
Adcote School For Girls, Shrewsbury

Another Day On The Street

The wind whistled through my hair while I wandered the streets of Brooklyn. I came across my favourite cafe; it sold freshly made golden-brown bagels with a nice, boiling coffee. I sat outside and picked up a crumpled newspaper, which was slightly smudged.

Waiting for my coffee to cool, I began reading when suddenly the newspaper flew out of my hands and landed gracefully on the floor. On it was a picture of a man. A wanted man. The one I was chasing. He was my brother!

Lucy Johnson (13)
Adcote School For Girls, Shrewsbury

Untitled

He was dead. I thought I stopped it all. I thought it would help. I pulled the trigger and, almost in slow motion, the bullet fired. He fell. But soon another rose, even worse than he was. The new order began under Himmler's rule. He waited till spring to invade Russia, and did it without a hitch. Then he set his sights on America and, just as easily, the Nazis took that too. For almost the past 50 years, we were living under the hell of Nazi rule and it was all my fault!

Alex Hughes (13)
Adcote School For Girls, Shrewsbury

Silence

I woke up in a sealed bag. I was taken out of the bag and led down a smelly corridor. I was thrown somewhere, and the door was slammed. I was alone. I felt around the wall, which was damp and wet. The walls were approximately one metre each way, one with a large door in the middle. I could hear noises from outside.

I didn't know where I was. How long would I be there? Suddenly, they opened the door, and I heard a gun's telltale click...

Rebecca Collins (13)
Adcote School For Girls, Shrewsbury

The Caretaker

It was a dark and cold night. Bobby was walking home past the graveyard where Mr Douglas worked. He saw the caretaker peering over a few graves. Bobby called out, asking if he was okay.
Suddenly Mr Douglas, the caretaker, jumped into a grave. Bobby thought it was strange so he went to investigate. Suddenly, Mr Douglas climbed out, covered in blood and eating something. Bobby shrieked. He covered his mouth and began to run. The caretaker was right behind him. Suddenly, Bobby ran into an alleyway but it was a dead end. He turned around, scared.

Caine Edmund Cawley (13)
Aldersley High School, Wolverhampton

Civil War!

Top regiment, including myself, were walking along, scouting the area when we heard a noise.

'Need to go check it out,' Remy said. Near the bush, a group of humans jumped out from both sides and took down two of my orc brothers!

I unsheathed my sword and swung it, severing one of their arms! Remy, Oki and I stood back-to-back. Jumping forward, a human slashed his sword, but missed and received a spear to the chest. We held the line fiercely, and eventually they retreated! Our land became ours again, and the humans stayed in theirs!

Kyle Onyx Skett (11)
Aldersley High School, Wolverhampton

Utopia

Once upon a time there was a magical world that was split in two. Humans, unicorns and fairies lived there. Everyone was rich, happy and peaceful. Until mysterious things began happening, that is. Animals were killed or stolen by something; something big. The humans went outside and began searching for the monster. They went to the other side of the world. It looked dark and cold because there were only moons, no suns. After a while, the humans found the monster hiding in some rocks. They gathered all the animals. They threw a massive rock at the monster. Dead.

Jake Aldersley (11)
Aldersley High School, Wolverhampton

Abandoned

My heart stopped for two seconds. I entered the orphanage, thinking how I could remake the building.
Smash!
I could hear shelves falling over, and I started to get worried. While going to investigate, I heard some sort of crying. It got louder and louder. But then, it quickly faded. I went back, but started to feel dizzy and hallucinate. Figures were flying past me. More and more and more. Then, right before me, a crumpled figure was moving forward slowly. Closer and closer. I froze in horror. Suddenly, it ran at me and I closed my eyes...

Matthew Baker (12)
Aldersley High School, Wolverhampton

Robotic End

One day, Johnny finally became old enough to play professional football for his hometown team 'Robotic Villains FC'. The downside to playing professional football was that everyone who did it had to be a robot. So Johnny underwent the procedure to turn him into a robot. Something went wrong however, and he began attacking the other robots. He told the audience to get rid of any and all robots because they were planning to take over! Everyone rose up and overthrew the robots, which had slowly been taking control of the governments for years!

Bradley David Newman (11)
Aldersley High School, Wolverhampton

Come Back On

Once upon a time there was a family on a distant, forested planet. Everything was relatively peaceful until one day the planet came under attack. It was the humans from the planet known as Earth! The family flew through the ruins of the city as it was being bombed, out to the canyon. They managed to get to the massive rocket there and they escaped the planet! They had nothing left but each other, but at least they had that. They cursed the notorious humans. They had destroyed their own planet and so they were taking others by force!

Sean Reeves (11)
Aldersley High School, Wolverhampton

The Smith's Story

Once upon a time, there was a small village. In Smith's village, everything was calm and peaceful. Fairies, hobbits and elves all lived happily. There was only one human; a woman named Sarah. One day, she and the elves went out to get their food. When they got back, they were shocked and upset to see that their village had been destroyed by a terrible dragon. All the other creatures had died. They fought the dragon, and with determination they managed to slay it. But nothing was ever the same in Smith's village after that.

Sophie Blakeway (11)
Aldersley High School, Wolverhampton

The Assassin

It was a scary day in the Madridian city of Lowhelse. I was doing my normal duty, defending the walls. Word had come through to the general that they were about to attack. Suddenly, they appeared out of the bushes below. We all began firing, but they were more accurate. My fellow guards fell down around me but I managed to get away. I ran through the houses, desperate to escape. I found myself surrounded by the enemy. The leader challenged me to a fight. I accepted. We fought fiercely, but I won and demanded that the troops leave.

Leon Flynn (11)
Aldersley High School, Wolverhampton

The Moon Began To Glitch

It was Christmas: the day of joy, happiness and gifts. We were going Christmas shopping. My parents and I went in our flying car to our favourite supermarket. I picked a cool outfit. It was a glow-in-the-dark dress.
I saw very tiny sparks coming from the moon, but I took no notice. Suddenly, the moon disappeared for a few minutes and came back again! Everybody panicked as we realised that the world we lived in wasn't real. It was a computer simulation! We needed to find a way out, but that was easier said than done...

Zilan Abdulla (11)
Aldersley High School, Wolverhampton

Dear Diary...

It was a shallow day. My world collapsed. Was anything real? My general was sending us to war; it didn't feel right. As we headed towards the gloomy, dead land, I sprinted out of line and headed for cover. Then I saw it. The murder of my friends, brothers even. Killed in seconds by... things. Suddenly, claws dug into my back. The shock of it triggered my anger. I turned around and shot it. I survived that dreadful day, but nobody else did. I knew it was only a matter of time before they took over, and now they have!

Anni Clarke-Shannon
Aldersley High School, Wolverhampton

The War Zone Patch!

It was a dark, deadly evening in the war zone. The pile of dead bodies was higher than ever before. It was sickening. My stomach was turning like a washing machine. The guns were still going strong. I peeked over the postbox, and ducked quickly as a bullet whizzed past my ear. The aliens had come in hordes and the human race's militaries were defeated within days. I was one of only a few survivors and I knew I needed to get back to the group. I quickly dashed through the houses and regrouped with them, ready for the revolution!

Jacob Smith (12)
Aldersley High School, Wolverhampton

The Ending

Once, there was a mad scientist who wanted to create the first real zombie, but it went wrong! All the other scientists were amazed at first. It was kept in a seemingly secure facility, but it eventually escaped! It infected everyone at the base and, slowly, the world was taken over by the virus. Eventually, there were only two people left in the world. They came up with a plan to defeat the zombie menace once and for all. They found a nuclear submarine and fired all the missiles out of it. Then they prepared for the end...

Cianan Duncombe (11)
Aldersley High School, Wolverhampton

My Future

I woke up after being knocked out. The light was glaring in my eyes. I looked up and saw a golden castle. As I walked up the narrow street, I saw elf-like creatures selling bread and fruit. I didn't know where I was. I arrived at the castle and saw golden statues of mystic, ancient gods! As the crested doors opened, I saw a massive throne. And sitting there was no other than... me! I couldn't believe my eyes. I fainted onto the floor. I woke up in a dark jail cell. *What is happening?* I thought.

Alexander Gilpin (11)
Aldersley High School, Wolverhampton

World Of Z

Zombies approached the dark city. They killed most of the people, but some of them grouped together and survived with food and weapons. There was a lonely boy who was trying to get help, and he suddenly heard something. It was getting closer and closer; his heart was pumping fast. The zombies turned the corner ahead of him and he ran for his life! They were slower, but relentless. He managed to find an abandoned warehouse and lock the shutters. Unfortunately, one of the zombies saw him and started tearing at the shutters!

Aro Hassan (11)
Aldersley High School, Wolverhampton

The Under Wonderland

I woke up one morning and jumped out of bed. For some reason, everything was chocolate. I really liked it; it was amazing. I couldn't believe it. I was so happy that I ran and ate as much as I could, but there was just so much! Then, I went outside and the whole world changed! Everything burned me to the touch and nightmarish creatures plagued the land. I remember thinking to myself that it was just a sick game. And it was. When I finally escaped, I interrogated the Creators and found out that I was just an experiment!

Vina Mahmood (12)
Aldersley High School, Wolverhampton

Killer Forest

Once upon a time there was a dark forest where humans, trolls and other mystical creatures lived.

One day, I received hundreds of threat letters because I accidentally killed one of the talking trees, thinking it was a normal one. Lots of people came to kill me that night and I escaped to my underground base with my weapons. They broke in and I opened fire, killing a few of them. Some of them escaped and told the other creatures and humans what had happened, and from that day on, everybody hated trollkind!

Owen Aulton (11)
Aldersley High School, Wolverhampton

The Crisis City

Hewgred was a creepy, cruel man. The city was full of lava and littered with destroyed buildings and pathways. Timmy South and his best friend, Shrew, always searched the grounds near the scorching lava. Hewgred hated this and he sent out his hounds after the boys. They ran away and the hounds fell into the lava. This infuriated Hewgred and he went outside. He ran over to the boys and was about to punish them, when the townsfolk showed up. They were sick of him and they pushed him into the lava! The planet was safe again!

Damian-Jake Fisher (11)
Aldersley High School, Wolverhampton

The Boat/Plane Crash

The plane tried to land and it crashed on the seahorse-shaped boat. It blew up and the mermaid started shouting. The seahorse boat sunk into the dark brown chocolate ocean. The survivors regrouped on the nearby island. Sadly, the mermaid wasn't one of them. They held a memorial in her honour for getting them that far. They wondered if anyone aboard the boat had survived. After weeks of living on the island, it became clear to them that nobody had. It was a tough world, but they got through the hard times together.

Kieron John Cawley (11)
Aldersley High School, Wolverhampton

If It Was Like This

A young boy named Edward was walking, when he tripped and kept falling! He fell for miles through a purple vortex and was teleported to another planet in the middle of a war! He was looked at by everyone as if he was an alien! He learned that the people there, who were all green, were at war with a zombie horde! They had pushed the horde back, but if they didn't win the next battle, all would be lost! Edward agreed to help and he chose his weapons and got ready. He looked over the trench and began shooting!

Sam Quinton (12)
Aldersley High School, Wolverhampton

The Tale Of The Furious Destroyer

Once upon a time there was a village deep in a dense forest. There were fourteen houses, with twenty-eight villagers total. There were only two guards, and one night they fell asleep at their post. When they woke up, the village was on fire and everybody was dead! The zombie horde had arrived three days ahead of their expectation! The guards fought through the zombies and retreated to the nearest village, warning them all. They successfully fought off the army of undead and reclaimed the planet!

Jamie Pilsbury (11)
Aldersley High School, Wolverhampton

The Door

My mum was shouting at me to go back. But I was already running. I couldn't stop. I reached it. As I was sucked in through the portal, a whirl of colour raced around me. A woman dressed in gold and white stood in front of me.
'You came from the other world?' she asked suspiciously.
'Yes, who are you?' I asked.
'I'm Queen Jaskiran of Saph,' she replied.
The world was magical and had everything I had ever dreamed of. I lived my whole life there!

Siobhan Dorrance (12)
Aldersley High School, Wolverhampton

Game Over

We were taken through the dense, thick jungle to a lab, where Leo planned his world dominance. He was going to be a morphing man, who changed into different creatures in order to tackle every government in their weak spot. I knew that that would be extremely bad and so I broke through the steel door with Echo, my friend. Leo was sitting there, in his natural form. He turned around as I fired my gun. He began to change, but it was too late. The bullet pierced him and he fell back, dead. His tyranny was over!

Kyle James Logan (11)
Aldersley High School, Wolverhampton

Sakurasina: The Island Of Death

Hashirasa, the demon king, was revived one day by the Yang gang and it was up to Squad Savage to save Kashira Island. Prisma, the rabbit goddess, used the Millenium Staff to seal the super volcano. Hashirasa broke out however, and started wreaking havoc on the island. The Savage Squad regrouped and charged at the giant monster. They attacked him fiercely and he fell to his knees. They gave him a chance to live if he accepted their terms and he agreed, sinking back into the volcano for eternity.

Darya Kakai (11)
Aldersley High School, Wolverhampton

Candy Land

It was a boring day at school and a young girl was sitting tiredly in her seat. With her head in her hands, the young girl started to slowly fall asleep. As her eyes closed, her mind began to picture a magical land. Soon the image was clear. She could see a land full of candy and unicorns. She heard her name. She frantically turned around to see a vast, golden gummy bear standing right there! Her eyes lit up like stars. The gummy bear sent her on a quest... Suddenly, she heard her name and woke up!

Gracie-Rae Osborn (11)
Aldersley High School, Wolverhampton

Falling Or Climbing

I took one step into the salty sea, the sand tickling my toes. Suddenly, I felt the earth shaking and I was swallowed up into the ground! The world went black. An amazing world, filled with all kinds of wonderful things. Clouds rained fairy dust and all the trees were waving at me. I knew I had to get back, even if it was perfect there. I climbed a cliff until I reached the surface, digging my way through the ground into the ocean. Spluttering, I grinned, knowing I had just been to another dimension.

Leah Ariel McInnis (11)
Aldersley High School, Wolverhampton

The Coldest Winter

I was at the peak of the mountain, sitting there as the snow covered the area around me. I rose up and walked back into my cave. 'I guess no one is coming,' I sigh... I am the Yeti. I have the title 'the Yeti' because I am the last of my kind, the rest died. Every day I go to the mountain to see if there are yetis but there never are, sadly. This was the last day of me trying, now I have stopped. I have now accepted the fact that I am the last yeti.

Leroy Uche (13)
Aldersley High School, Wolverhampton

Six Feet Under

Fatigued, I drove cautiously up the steep, rocky hill to my mansion. Stepping out of my Rolls Royce, the cold breeze hit me. I made myself a cup of lemon tea in my house. I started pacing around the room, thinking of all the investigations dealt with that day. Sounds were rushing through my head. I strolled outside, and suddenly everything went dark around me and I was subsiding. I blacked out, and when I woke up I found myself in a coffin six feet under, and nowhere to go!

Oumou Kesso Barry (12)
Aldersley High School, Wolverhampton

Not A Girl's Dream

Lilly just had the worst night ever. She had just spilt gravy on her mum's boss. She was sent to her room.
'I wish I could live on a farm,' she murmured.
The next day, Lilly found herself lying in a puddle of mud, with slobber on her from the panting dog above her face. She looked around. She was on a massive farm! It was stinky though, and she didn't like it at all. She cried and wished to be back home. The next morning, she woke up in her own room!

Priya Kaur Rayet (11)
Aldersley High School, Wolverhampton

Hope

Hurtling into space, the fiery earth became smaller and smaller. The year was 2216. Planet Earth as we knew it ended. Looking back, we regretted what we had done. It was all our fault. Everything was burned, but some people survived. We named the new planet Hope.
Now, in 2546, the planet is filled with lush, green vegetation and sacred animals! We made a vow before cryosleep that we would never harm the planet, and now we must keep the promise!

Matthew Bickerton (11)
Aldersley High School, Wolverhampton

Man's Hell 2055

The future was supposed to be good. Instead of birds gliding through the sky, there were bullets. We had to live day-to-day with savages watching our every move, as if it was normal! The fall of civilisation led to the complete collapse of any form of peace between groups of humans. Every morning, I woke up to the sound of conflict, sometimes far away, most of the time not. The once-blue sky had been transformed into a coal-black colour. It was man's hell. Until we escaped...

Niamh Clarke-Shannon (12)
Aldersley High School, Wolverhampton

The Battle Of The Unicorns And Fairies

The year was 4040 in the land of Imagination. Unicorns had lived peacefully, until then. The evil fairies took all the fun out of everything, and they even took the horns off the unicorns! They lived for months under the oppression of the fairies. One day, a small band of rebel unicorns stormed the fairies' castle and captured all of them! They demanded their horns back and, scared, the fairy king obliged. The fairies were made to leave the land, and it went back to being perfect!

Jamie Passmore (11)
Aldersley High School, Wolverhampton

Creatures Of Up There

A figure was heading my way. It didn't exactly look human, but it had to be, didn't it? I walked cautiously forwards, unsure whether I was making a mistake. It came into view. I screamed. It hissed. I dashed past the cosy houses, spotting a BMW and hiding behind it. I looked up, and it was right there! It licked what should have been its lips. I scrambled away, found a pipe wrench and beat it to death! Shaken up, I ran away to warn the others of what was lurking on our planet!

Tyler John David Preece (15)
Aldersley High School, Wolverhampton

M&M Land

Once upon a time a boy dreamed of living in a world of M&Ms. They were his favourite sweets. After his dream ended, he realised that he was no longer in Wolverhampton, but M&M land! His dream had come true. He ran around, eating as many M&Ms as he could, but after about ten minutes he began to get bored. There was nobody else in M&M land and the chocolate tasted very bland after a while. He cried for hours and suddenly woke up back in his bed!

Samuel Nestor (11)
Aldersley High School, Wolverhampton

Moon?

It was a starry night. The only thing in sight was a distant glow of white. The town was quiet, deserted and mysterious. A girl sat on a bench, doing nothing. Nothing at all. That girl was me. I wanted some alone time. My family thought I was crazy, weird and mysterious; However, I was just different. I believed in ghosts. They used to call me crazy! That day, I saw the strangest thing. The moon flickered off, and then back on. Something wasn't right with it...

Gabriella Farrier (8)
Aldersley High School, Wolverhampton

Dark Days

My heart thumped in my chest. I saw miserable people walking around. I even saw my grandad, who had recently passed away. My only feeling was despair. The town was all smashed into pieces as the undead left their mark on it. I turned around and saw about ten of them heading my way! I ran and ran, but they always seemed to be right there. I gave up. They were about to get me!
Suddenly, I woke up; the beautiful sunlight gently grazing my eyes. It was just a dream!

Holly Lane (12)
Aldersley High School, Wolverhampton

Podge's Place

'Welcome,' said some lovely-smelling gingerbread men. I was so surprised to see them speaking to me. Was it a dream? I followed them through a lovely-smelling candyfloss tree forest. As the trees waved at me, I felt warmth in my heart; happiness. They took me across a chocolate lake and through a cave covered in jelly beans. All I could see was darkness now. I heard a cackle, and suddenly, the trees were gone. They had been replaced by evil, grinning demons!

Paige Susan Noble (11)
Aldersley High School, Wolverhampton

The Final Warning...

Walking through the portal, she was placed in another world... At first, it seemed like an impeccable world; but she was very wrong... the place was lined with chocolate, even the roads. She began to eat, but she stopped and looked around for the first real time. There where bodies lying everywhere, crashed cars inside of buildings. No sign of life was present... She suddenly woke up, she heard an unfamiliar voice which said: 'You have been warned...'

Nikola Armale (11)
Aldersley High School, Wolverhampton

Untitled

Rapidly, the ground began shaking! Anthony and I were really scared. We thought it was an earthquake. Finally, the floor split as if opening a door to hell, and we fell down! We landed in some water and looked around. There were strange creatures everywhere. They hissed at us and we realised they were vampires! Luckily, we had some UV lights on us from science class and burned them all! We found a ladder at the back of the cave and climbed up to safety!

Mathew Wynne Jones (11)
Aldersley High School, Wolverhampton

Quick Scary Fiasco

On a typical dark night, just like every night, two adventurers were sitting on a crystal black and white bench watching crime after crime occur. Suddenly, the ground started shaking and an enormous beast appeared from behind a building. The beast screeched and breathed purple flames out of its mouth. Everybody ran for their lives, except for the adventurers. They pulled out their sword and ran towards the monster. They killed it and saved the city!

Eniola Raheem (13)
Aldersley High School, Wolverhampton

Tropicana

Once upon a time there was a world full of polite people. Except for one man, of course. Josh hated everyone and everyone feared him. One day, everyone went round to his house and begged him to be polite like them. He was reluctant at first until Jack, his only friend among the population, stepped forward. He told Josh that he didn't need to hate anyone any more. He listened to him and apologised to everyone, becoming a much nicer person!

Ben Walker (11)
Aldersley High School, Wolverhampton

Winder

I slowly opened my eyes and realised my feet were covered in a layer of thick, black smoke. I stood up and looked around. I noticed that the smoke was getting hotter by the minute. Then I saw something in the distance. Curious, I ran towards the figure. When I was only a few feet away, it turned around. It had glowing red eyes and was growling at me. I sprinted away, the monster hot on my heels. It was the apocalypse!

Amanda Ward (11)
Aldersley High School, Wolverhampton

Aqua Sea

We all lived under the sea. All five million of us. We were running out of resources, and we mined frantically day and night for more, making the supply scarcer and scarcer. One day, I had an idea. I told everyone and they reluctantly agreed, glad that someone had an idea. We went to the surface and found out that we could breathe! We walked out onto the land and began our new lives on the bountiful surface world!

Fletcher Rushbury (12)
Aldersley High School, Wolverhampton

Welcome To Wonderland

I remember it was ten years (not because I have a good memory, but because I saw the tattered and torn calendar on the wall), ten whole years since I first came here. The giant amusement park sign imprinted with the words *Welcome To Wonderland*, now I see how ironic that is. In reality it was the complete opposite of the name. You see I was on the Ferris wheel when... it stopped. Nothing new, it always happens. Until the outbreak happened; all of the prisoners, all them monsters escaped. The suspense of living on the edge. For ten years.

Noah Green (12)
Bishop Vesey's Grammar School, Sutton Coldfield

Disasterville

The morning newspaper was laid across the table as my brother came down the stairs. The title was predictable: 'Another Dead'. There were fifteen people in the town. Eight were heartless killers and the other seven were unlucky innocents. Nobody knew who the killers were. Not even the killers themselves. It was all a government experiment. They wiped our minds after we killed, so we couldn't possibly remember. I knew in my heart that I had killed someone, but it depressed me that I couldn't remember who, when or why.

Charles Michael Fortescue Hubbard (12)
Bishop Vesey's Grammar School, Sutton Coldfield

The Lonely Light

In a deep, dark universe, not too far from ours, light didn't exist. Well, that's what the Lelotions thought. They were the ghostly inhabitants of the Gluto planet; which was just like Pluto, except much bigger. However, the Lelotions were wrong. The light had been stolen by one of their own, thousands of years before. He had stored it in a chest in his mansion, wanting it all for himself. One day, his descendant decided that it was time to stop being selfish and he opened the chest, releasing bright light back into the sky!

Thomas Cartmill (11)
Bishop Vesey's Grammar School, Sutton Coldfield

Untitled

*Today, the world is Utopia, and world peace has occurred.
Everyone is happy, unlike in the past...*
I put down my pen and looked around. The bulky man with
black glasses and a simple suit covering that sickly, pale
skin, released the gun from my head. His veins looked like a
spider's web, showing through his skin.
It wasn't true, there was no Utopia. The world was coming
to an end, but the government were forcing me to write
that so they could escape the planet without being hunted
down and killed!

Mackenzie Davis (13)
Bishop Vesey's Grammar School, Sutton Coldfield

Don't Panic

If you're reading this, you're probably from a groggy, primitive planet that has only just discovered intergalactic propulsion. You might even think you're clever for it. Nope! If you're travelling at the speed of light, it would take you four years to get to Proxima Centauri, so stop staring at your digital watches and invent the FTL engine already! For more information, please visit the Alpha Centauri system, where the Vogons will be happy to give you a transdimensional link to the Mouselands or Magrathea!

Joshua Tranchant (12)
Bishop Vesey's Grammar School, Sutton Coldfield

The TV

Edward was watching 'The Fantastic Four.' He had been sick the previous day and had stayed home from school. The scene changed to a different dimension.
Hiss!
Smoke began to pour out the sides of the TV.
When the smoke cleared, he was standing in a strange place. The sky was red and the trees appeared to be made of glass. The ground was purple. Fleshy maggots writhed and crawled all over his feet. Edward screamed and yellow smoke poured out of his mouth!

Ishan Mitra
Bishop Vesey's Grammar School, Sutton Coldfield

Destruction Of Zarg!

Another explosion destroyed a section of the hundred-foot wall. Several evacuation ships lifted off, only to be sucked into the hurricane that was about to destroy Zarg. Zarg was a swamp planet, covered in miles of bogs and dense rainforests. In one of the forests, the first inhabitants of the planet had established their home. Only fifty years later, it was all destroyed by the interstellar hurricane that was sweeping through the universe, taking every living thing out of existence...

Matthew Merrill (11)
Bishop Vesey's Grammar School, Sutton Coldfield

The End

The dark, grey, gloomy clouds peered over the dull world. There were scavengers scattered everywhere; some looking more depressed than others because of the world coming to its end. Meanwhile, the sun moved ever closer at a slow pace. The sun. It was a fluorescent lava colour, which glowed brightly. Five hours later, people gathered together to say their goodbyes. Some were able to leave on advanced rocket ships, bound for Mars. Anyone who wasn't rich was doomed to die...

Thomas James Green (12)
Bishop Vesey's Grammar School, Sutton Coldfield

Untitled

There was nothing in the universe, absolutely nothing. Blacker than you could imagine black being. During this time, there was another universe, far away. And it was at war. Swords swung menacingly for the right to rule. Bodies laid sprawled out helplessly and blood oozed from the flesh. Peace was in the past. Painful screams were heard across the system. Whoever won would control the Universemaker and create their own universe! That universe would become our own!

Ethan Finney (12)
Bishop Vesey's Grammar School, Sutton Coldfield

The Crooked, Evil-Casted Island

The beautiful, green trees on the haunted island were being incised, and there was no hope of righteousness being instated in the evil parallel universe! The Hook pirates were highly sinister and their greediness grew, just like their attitude towards us sluggish slaves. Out of nowhere, a hideous noise of gunfire commenced and I went to see what was going on. An uprising! I grabbed a gun and joined the fight. The Hooks had had their day, it was going to be our turn...

Vraj Tushar Shah (13)
Bishop Vesey's Grammar School, Sutton Coldfield

The Multiverse

The multiverse was a vast place where all of the many diverse, elemental universes were. Those realms could be beautiful gardens, dark abysses or chaotic post-apocalyptic disasters. There was a great sorcerer named Darkotron, who had been turned evil by the Darkverse. He sought to control the whole multiverse! Mr E was his nemesis, and they had a massive fight one day. Mr E managed to defeat Darkotron and free the multiverse from his grasp!

James Foxall (12)
Bishop Vesey's Grammar School, Sutton Coldfield

Untitled

A dystopian world, slowly falling to its knees like a beheaded traitor. The dry world consumes you as everyone clings to the land for a sip of water. Humanity is on the brink of extinction.

It all began in the evil hearts of those who had it all. The government controlled all of the money, and hefty taxes and bills drained most people just like that. Slowly, greed took over the world and it became what it is today...

Oliver Henry Gray-Nimmo (13)

Bishop Vesey's Grammar School, Sutton Coldfield

The Future Is Chrome!

Everything was chrome when I visited the future. It was so shiny and bright that it was almost impossible to see! I guess that was why everyone wore shades! I was accidentally transported to the future after going over the speed limit in an 80s hatchback. Chrome cars hovered in the polluted sky above me, and even people's clothes were chrome! Suddenly, I woke up in my bed in 2017. It was all just a dream!

Leon Lwanga
Bishop Vesey's Grammar School, Sutton Coldfield

Corona

There they were. The trio was waiting patiently, hidden by the thick foliage. A cold draught sliced their necks like a sword blade. Smirking, Maximillian, Jamie and Sofie took out the equipment. Quietly, the group waited for Kasparian's signal to proceed.

After an hour of waiting, an eerie voice came through Max's intercom.

'Go ahead.'

Cautiously, the team set up the device. Finally, it was ready. The bomb was ready.

'Three, two, one...'

Kaboom!

The explosion threw the group backwards. All that was heard was an ear-piercing shriek, like a blackboard being scratched. The dictator was gone!

Yehia Shawkat (13)
Concord College, Shrewsbury

Nature's Wrath

Lucy was lost and scared in the forest. Warily, she walked deeper until light couldn't penetrate the dense foliage. Her eyes adjusted to the gloom and she saw luminescent fireflies floating towards her. Fascination turned into agony as they burrowed into her soft, delicate flesh. Screaming, she fled, stumbling through serpentine-like ivy which entwined her and dragged her down. Lucy felt the ground pounding and saw a humanoid tree-golem thundering towards her, with a limb honed to a sharp point. Lucy scrambled for her life, but before she could reach the ground she felt the deadly, spear-like branch impale her...

Penri William Edward Jones (13)
Concord College, Shrewsbury

The Price Of Perfection

'Genetically modified?' I ask my mother.

'No... you're... it's reversible, and we're going to start reversing it as soon as we can,' she replies. The rest of the Resistance stands huddled around me, whispering and waiting for me to say something. Something has changed about the way I see them. They no longer blur together, under their bulletproof armour they are all individuals, but they all share the same purpose. Suddenly, they all fall silent. I am about to ask why, when the wall behind me collapses, and the room is engulfed in flames.

Eden Skye Broadbent (13)

Concord College, Shrewsbury

What's Really Right?

Crouching behind one of the few bushes left in Scaldra, I noticed that one of the dragons circling the tree was limping. There were three in total, all with shiny scales. The one that was limping was smaller than the other two. I reckoned it must have been two parents with their child. Mark must have been thinking the same, because he looked more sorrowful than usual.

'The sooner we do this, the better,' I said.

I pulled out my gun and took one last look at the creatures. 'Is it better for them?' Mark asked...

Rose Smith (13)
Concord College, Shrewsbury

Crimson

When people interfere with the preservation of a race, it never goes well. A fluke accident of desired immortality went terribly wrong. It turned everyone into what I can only describe as monsters; bloodthirsty demons who killed everything they saw. I was the only survivor! I had two options: lose my humanity or lose my life. A brutal darkness surrounded me. I shivered as a cold breath caressed my neck like a knife. I turned to see crimson eyes, full of hunger. The creature bore its teeth at me! I grabbed my gun and killed it!

Olivia Marcham (13)
Concord College, Shrewsbury

Survivor

Silence. It unnerved me. A few moments ago I was being chased down by them. But now there was only silence. I tried to get a grip on things. I was the only human left. My home, Earth, was destroyed. A few of us moved to Earth Alpha, but soon the savages of the planet turned on us and killed everyone except for me. I shouldn't have survived, but I did. They were coming after me. I felt a hand grab my shoulder and I screamed. It was another human! How? We ran to safety...

T'Oluwafe Eyifewa Onadele (13)
Concord College, Shrewsbury

The Struggle

'Can I do this? Should I do this? What will happen to me afterwards? Will the police find out?'
'Yes, you can do this! They killed your brother! You'll be fine, just as long as you succeed. And the police can't find out if there are no police!'
Brian agreed with his friend. He wanted revenge for his brother's death, and this was a good way to get it. He turned the key, and the big red button popped up. He pressed it, nothing to lose any more...

Thomas Dix (14)
Concord College, Shrewsbury

Untrustworthy Friends

In the year 2666, humans had migrated from Earth to Neptune because all their water had evaporated thanks to radiation and pollution. Because of their actions, they had a visit from uninvited guests. Aliens came down and laid waste to much of the colony there.

I was just walking with my parents one day, and suddenly a massive spaceship flew down and fired lasers at us, killing them both. I breathed heavily and screamed. I vowed revenge on the evil invaders and took control of our armed forces. A year later, we crushed them under the might of our armoury!

Arthur Dimbylow (12)
Fairfield High School, Hereford

The Lost Island Of Elvesztett

Every night people were disappearing from Elvesztett. Once they had gone, they were never seen again. The people of the town decided that they were going to capture the culprit. The mayor, Mo, volunteered to stay out for the night to try to discover who was taking his people. His friend, Po, also stayed out with him just in case. Soon enough they saw a monstrous figure climbing over the wall, heading towards a house. Mo gave the signal, and the town's police force opened fire. The monster fell off the house and died! Elvesztett was safe again...

Kate Jessica Coupland (12)
Fairfield High School, Hereford

Warhammer 50,000 Fall Of Baal

In the year 50,000, the empire of man fell with its emperor. The forces of chaos ruled the galaxy, and nearly everyone became heretics, betraying their 'brethren' to obey the pantheon of Khone, Tzeench, Shanesh and Nurgle. The resistance was readying to fight. The odds were against them, but they had Leman, Vulcan and Sanguminus, the galaxy's greatest warriors. Sanguminus was leading the rebellion, and he was putting on his golden armour. His pale skin and his long, blonde hair gleamed in the sunlight. He was mankind's salvation...

Adam Smith (12)
Fairfield High School, Hereford

Alternate Universe

All was silent, not even the latest Hoverbots were around. The billboards weren't even lit. A figure appeared out of the fog in front of me. A familiar figure. The person I was waiting for. It was me! The cloning program had worked, but it had used all of the power in the city! I walked over to 'myself' and started talking. However, the clone didn't talk back. It just stood there, motionless. Suddenly, it reached into its coat and pulled out a gun! It pointed it at me.
The last words I heard were: 'Just me. Not you.'

Holly Prior (12)
Fairfield High School, Hereford

Speechless: Child Prodigy

Imogen and Connor were flying their ship for the first time. It jolted and jerked as they went into the atmosphere of the strange, new planet. They landed safely, and they unbuckled their harnesses. The gravity was very low there. They stepped out onto the surface, amazed at their discovery. Suddenly, they saw a shadow on the horizon. It was sprinting towards them. They didn't know what to do, so they got back on the ship. Unfortunately, it was incredibly strong and forced its way aboard. They cowered in fear as the monster advanced...

Beth Llewellin (12)
Fairfield High School, Hereford

Darkness Falls!

On a faraway planet, where robot people ruled and humans were enslaved, Clara was hiding from her robot masters in the castle. She couldn't take it any more. She was sick of being treated like she was nothing by the cold, emotionless overlords. She just wanted to see the light of the day and breathe fresh air for the first time in her life. She heard the guard stomp past and knew it was her only chance. She ran towards the window and leaped out of it into the fields below. She ran to the forest and joined the Resistance!

Maisie White (12)
Fairfield High School, Hereford

The Man In The Cape

There was a world once, not at all like ours. It was full of destruction and hatred. There was no escape, all because of the man in the cape. He came to their world when progress was at its peek. Before, sleek buildings. Now they're all destroyed, freedom is all they want. They're all slaves, working in the deep caves. Serving under the control of the man in the cape. They made a clan, to rise above this man. Charging towards his big, bold home, this world was their own! Controlled no more, now his body lies on the floor.

Lucas Marchant (13)
Fairfield High School, Hereford

The Big Discovery

I stumbled past a body and I shrieked with fear, turning swiftly into work mode. I ran towards the corpse, my long waistcoat slightly brushing the human remains. The head from the decapitated body was pinned to the wall, with blood dripping out. I began to inspect the scene. It wasn't the first time that a crime like that had occurred in that house. I realised that the door was locked from the inside when I barged in, so the killer must still be there...
It was then that I felt hot breath on the back of my neck!

Ella Gibbs (13)
Fairfield High School, Hereford

The Story Of Derek The Cat

A cat went to town and bought a cat toy. When he got home, he played with it. Suddenly, Derek bashed his head against the wall accidentally and the wall opened up, revealing a portal to another dimension. The cat was very confused. He went inside and, as quick as a flash, he was transported to another dimension. The world was full of cats. Not just any cats, however. Talking ones, like Derek! He was finally home. He had always wondered how he could speak English. He had never known his parents, but there they were!

Christiana Mills (13)
Fairfield High School, Hereford

A House In The Wood

The year was 1916. The war had been going on for two years. We stopped at an abandoned house in some random woods in Germany. Everything was fine, until we noticed that we weren't alone. We heard shuffling noises. At first we thought it was the Germans, but unfortunately it was much, much worse...

It started picking us off one by one. The monster. I only saw it once, when it was bearing down on me, ready to kill. Thankfully, I had my pistol and I killed it. We got out of the woods and never spoke of it again!

Bridget Elizabeth Morgan (12)
Fairfield High School, Hereford

The Investigator

He exited the train onto the derelict platform. He walked up to the telephone box that he had been instructed to use, so as to be untraceable by any tracing devices. Little did he realise, it was splattered in blood. He looked back at the train but it wasn't there... He charged at the doorway but it was blocked. Then he saw the windows. They were boarded and dripping with a viscous, red liquid. He froze in horror. He didn't notice the dark figure with red eyes approaching from behind him...

Daniel Smith (13)
Fairfield High School, Hereford

Troll Tree

The troll tree was a humongous tree where lots of little trolls lived. The branches swung in the breeze of the wind. Below, the child trolls were playing on the ground. Little did they know, there was a group of ogres nearby, watching them. They wanted to eat the trolls. They sneaked over to the edge of the long grass and waited till the trolls were asleep. They charged, screaming and shouting. Luckily, the trolls had befriended the tree and it came alive and stomped on the ogres until they gave up and retreated!

Lewis Lloyd (13)
Fairfield High School, Hereford

Alex And The Psychos!

I grabbed my Milrith sword from the counter and walked through the crowd of fellow 'psychos'. It was the rebellion versus the tyrannical government. They used propaganda against us, making us out to be crazy. That was the day that we took back our world. We stormed out of the bunker and were met with a hail of gunfire. We dived into the trenches and began fighting for our lives. Many men fell on both sides. We had the superior soldiers and we won, forcing the government to give control of everything to us!

Alexis Skye Powell (13)
Fairfield High School, Hereford

Zray's Rebellion

I went outside and was greeted by screams and dying people. I saw Zonkort, a prince, ordering his men to kill everyone. I ran to find my grandad, but then I remembered he had already left the village with the rest of my family. Everything was burning. Zonkort's men were destroying the whole neighbourhood. The town of Notune was going to be taken over by his army. I ran away, ashamed, but knowing there was nothing I could have done. I went to find my family, and we moved to another planet, safe at last!

Rudi Ambrose Davies (12)
Fairfield High School, Hereford

Untitled

One day, I went to the shops. I checked the sell-by date of some chicken, bought it and then walked out. I got back to my house and started cooking. Just then, I heard something outside my house. The whole ground shook as an explosion from across the street blew open all my windows! I ran to see what it was, and gasped in horror. UFOs were swooping down from the sky and firing lasers at the house! I ran to my rocket ship and took off, heading for another planet. I saw my house being destroyed behind me...

Dewi Meredith
Fairfield High School, Hereford

Untitled

It was a stormy night and the moon was shining bright. I had to go out and hunt for food, which was a great risk in this place. I grabbed my shotgun, took a deep breath and opened the bunker door. As soon as I stepped outside, I heard a scream. I sprinted to the noise. The creatures had found us! The indigenous predators of Neptune were vicious creatures and everyone was scared of them. They were attacking and killing my people. I had no choice but to run for my life, tears streaming down my face.

Aaron Pearson (13)
Fairfield High School, Hereford

The Endless Disease...

The pitch-black darkness filled the cold, uneasy atmosphere. The sound of fatal deaths lurked in the town, which laid thousands of miles beneath what was once a place of love and understanding. In the hospital, loud screams filled the halls as hundreds of patients were piled in every hour. Each and every one of them was carrying the vile, uncurable disease. With the infection spreading rapidly, the human race's days were numbered. I grinned. My handiwork was almost complete...

Evie White (12)
Fairfield High School, Hereford

Untitled

They were the size and shape of matches. Vulnerable, they panted for breath. Their world was destroyed. All it took was one step of a foot to destroy the mini town. The houses had collapsed. The worried survivors looked up at me, the giant who had destroyed their town. I was remorseful, and I wasn't even aware of what I was doing at the time. The evil queen had possessed me and made me do it! I explained that to the townspeople and agreed to help them overthrow the queen!

Lucy Baker (13)
Fairfield High School, Hereford

Alone

My mum left the house at around eleven that night. That's when it happened... I went up to my room to finish some homework, and then I heard it. Booming noises every few seconds, as if someone was hitting their head on something. It got louder and louder so I quickly locked my bedroom door and turned off the light. A shiver went down my back and I froze. I knew it was behind me.
It whispered, 'Don't worry, no one will hear you die.'

Jasmine Jefferson (13)
Fairfield High School, Hereford

The Last Stand In Naziland

We have been planning this day for seventy-one years.
Enough waiting. Hitler had won World War II and his
generals control every aspect of our lives. They renamed
Earth 'Naziland' and killed anyone who, even accidentally,
called it otherwise. Factories now cover what was once
countryside, and there is so much smog that all wildlife has
completely perished. Today is the day we rise up as a
community. We take back our land *today.*

Fred Davies (12)
Fairfield High School, Hereford

The Door

The door I had walked through had disappeared. I didn't know how to get back home. I knew I had to find the door. Slowly, I walked past a river into some woods. I continued walking, not knowing where I was going or which world I was on. I heard a crunch behind me. I looked around, but saw nothing. I breathed a sigh of relief and turned back around. I gasped. A massive, lumbering figure was towering above me!

Faith Roberts (12)
Fairfield High School, Hereford

A World Full Of Weird And Wonderful Things Which Happen!

In a far away world, something weird and wonderful happened. One day, the creatures began to act strangely. Everybody was baffled and half of the townspeople went searching for the source. Eventually, they found a small cave. They went inside and were shocked to find a witch practising her incantations. She was angry, but noticed that the townspeople were angrier. She asked them what the matter was. It turned out that she had been saying a spell wrong. She wanted to cook using magic, but accidentally possessed the animals! They all laughed about it and the animals returned to normal!

Ellie Tyler (13)
Madeley Academy, Telford

What If?

As the wind howled and the rain thudded against the window, Ben had the weirdest dream. He could hear what sounded like a plane engine. He jumped up off the sofa and headed into the kitchen. He reached the back door and the sound grew louder and louder. He cautiously opened the door and a bright light filled his eyes.
'Don't Skarta, let the earthling go,' a strange voice said.
The light vanished and Ben was astounded to see two aliens walking into their spaceship! They took off.
Suddenly, Ben woke up!

Joshua James Allen (13)
Madeley Academy, Telford

Mercury Survivor

There was once a war over Mercury. Nobody could set foot on the surface because it was too close to the sun and they would be burned. Special buildings were constructed so the armies could fight in them. The special force from Earth (known as UNSA) was sent down to the building. They encountered the aliens that they were supposed to fight, and opened fire. The aliens didn't stand a chance against such an elite force and the alien commander surrendered! The members of UNSA were given special medals for their services to Earth!

Dylan Harris (12)
Madeley Academy, Telford

Untitled

The mist rose up to the dark, dull sky. Wind blew across the tall trees, making them shiver. The menacing fog grew bigger and denser until it was impossible for Cory to see. The house was quiet. Cory walked slowly into the house. As he crept up the stairs, the bedroom door opened. Standing there was a mysterious figure. Cory froze in horror and then suddenly ran for his life. He knew the monster would be right behind him, and it was! He turned around and saw the shine of the monster's teeth as it bore down upon him!

Ethan Green (12)
Madeley Academy, Telford

From One To Another

I quickly ran towards my bedroom door after hearing a faint knock. My door swung open fast. I couldn't believe it, there was an actual desert in front of me. I nervously stepped out into the hot, abandoned desert. I heard my bedroom door close behind me, it also disappeared! I tried using my phone, but there was no signal. I wandered around the desert, looking for another living human. All I could see were corpses. Suddenly, a hand reached down from the heavens and plucked me from the sandy deathtrap. I woke up at home!

Courtney Jade Edgar (13)
Madeley Academy, Telford

The Remains

He bashed open the rusting metal door and locked it shut behind him. Dust and sand covered the room. The sound of footsteps outside alerted him to the presence of the military surrounding him. He knew he had to reach the safe zone in time if he wanted to live. With his last remaining ounce of strength, he broke the window and ran on the rooftops next to him. Machine guns rattled all around him and bullets whizzed past him. He slid down off a roof into a river, letting the current take him far away from that place.

Jamie George Morris (13)
Madeley Academy, Telford

What Really Happened In Class 8.4A

It was just a normal day at first. Dan was just walking into school for his first lesson. As he walked into the English corridor, he heard howls, screams and moans and saw flashing lights coming from inside his classroom. The noises got louder as he approached. He swung open the door and saw a ravenous werewolf, feeding on what was left of the teacher. Dan walked in, ready to face the beast. He did not realise that there was another one crouched under a desk near the entrance... Dan was never seen again!

Isabelle Edney (13)
Madeley Academy, Telford

A New Life Begins

It was a nice sunny day and it was my first day at secondary school. I went to a few lessons, and then suddenly everything changed around me! I was on an empty street, with only a few houses on. The landscape looked different. I read a newspaper and discovered that it was the year 1605! I didn't know what to do, so I just walked around exploring. There was no electricity, not even fresh water! I hated the place and wished to be back at school. Abruptly, I woke up in class!

Caitlyn Webb (12)
Madeley Academy, Telford

Untitled

Once, there was an island filled with ghosts and sausages. One day, a rocket landed on island, where humans weren't allowed. The sausages weren't happy about that and they attacked the people. The people on board the rocket were shocked to see a bunch of talking sausages attacking them. They had an idea. They activated their boosters and fire sprayed out at the sausages, cooking them! The humans were happy about that because they had forgotten to bring their food!

Warren Whittaker (12)
Madeley Academy, Telford

Nothing Is Perfect!

One ordinary day, everyone was having fun. Children were playing and the adults were relaxing. Superman and the Hulk were patrolling the city. Suddenly, they turned a corner and spotted the Joker! The Joker turned around and laughed, disappearing before their very eyes. The next day, he caused havoc in the city, blowing up buildings and robbing shops. Luckily, Superman showed up and beat him up. Then he took the Joker to jail, where he stayed forever!

Isabel Black (11)
Madeley Academy, Telford

The Discovery And Destruction Of Halo

There was a wheezing, groaning noise, and out of nowhere the TARDIS materialised. The Doctor came out and saw an armoured figure standing in front of him. He asked it who it was and it said that its name was Master Chief. They looked out of the window at a planet surrounded by ships.

The Doctor said, 'Which planet is that? And who are they?'

'That is Halo, and they are Covenant ships,' Master Chief replied.

The Pillar of Autumn began attacking the ships. Master Chief and The Doctor fought off the covenant, saving Halo!

Dylan Livingston (13)

Shrewsbury Academy, Shrewsbury

Untitled

Suddenly, the mountains dropped away, revealing a vast swathe of forest. Stormrider's muscled sides rippled under his legs, each beat of his wings buffeting him with cool air. Far below, a herd of deer bounced across a stream, and from the trees burst an enormous cat. It wasn't chasing the deer however. From behind him came a rumbling. The new world was alive! Stormrider looked; an avalanche began cascading down the mountain. He flew down and rescued the big cat, flying it to safety just in time!

Lucia Malvone (13)
Shrewsbury Academy, Shrewsbury

The Devil's Playhouse

I was stuck in a massive playhouse. I explored, unsure of how I got here or how to get out. I looked out of the window. Below me was a massive fiery pit. Suddenly, a pair of scarlet eyes appeared in the window. A laughing face. The most demonic face ever. I realised what had happened. I died and since I had behaved poorly in life, I was stuck in Hell for eternity. The Devil reached in and picked me up, making me move. I was completely helpless.

Kyle Williams (12)
The Aconbury Centre, Hereford

The Swirling Hole

It was a stormy night and I was in an old house. The door started screeching. I was scared. It was like I was in another dimension. It smelled like an old funeral home. I didn't know where I was. I didn't really know where. I had just been walking along a path, when suddenly the ground swallowed me up and I was teleported there! The house was an old style, but looked fairly new. I didn't know if I was in the past or the future!

Kieron Clements (12)
The Aconbury Centre, Hereford

The Battle Of Myths

Shining brightly, the sun gleamed over the two worlds. The humans and the gods were working together in perfect harmony. Suddenly, a mythical dragon appeared out of nowhere! It started causing destruction to the human world! The gods decided to intervene and they combined their powers into one supercharged beam. They loaded it into Cupid's bow and fired it at the dragon. It let out a mighty roar as the beam of fire, water, electricity and many other elements hit it square in the face. It collapsed, dead!

Mark Dixon (14)
The Burton Borough School, Newport

A Dream Come True

Once, a girl named Skye went into her room and opened her bookcase. She saw a book glowing pink and her mouth opened in shock. She had never seen it before! She opened it and a bright light sprang out! She was transported to a magical world! It was everything she liked: flowers, horses and chocolate! She skipped through the fields, singing her favourite song!

When she had had enough, she found the book and went back to her room. She visited the world often and made many friends there.

Jessica Broome (12)
The Burton Borough School, Newport

The End Of The World

Screaming. Endless screaming was all I heard as I woke on that day. I saw the darkness clouding the city. More screams and then silence. I didn't know what was happening. Then I saw it. It was made of black smoke and had an orange face. It stared at me, hungry for my untouched soul. I was not corrupted; the only one left. I began to run, but it appeared in front of me. I sank to my knees. It reached out a hand and took my soul. A few seconds of blackness and then I felt... nothing.

Jacob Johnson (14)
The Burton Borough School, Newport

Welcome To Wonderland

Jessie and Jacob fell into the woods, stumbling and tripping! They landed near a small oak tree. They didn't know where they were now. They were disoriented, but began walking. They came to a strange gate in the middle of the forest and opened it. When they went inside, they noticed a lot of strange things! There were plants and animals that they had never seen before and the small, gated community they had stepped into appeared to be populated by elves! They were confused at first, but soon became overjoyed as they realised what they had discovered!

Emily Bell (11)
The Kingsley School For Girls, Leamington Spa

Welcome To Wonderland

Alex and Tina fell faster and faster. The book had swallowed them whole. They looked in amazement. They could see the bottom of the pages. They screamed. Suddenly, they landed on a rotten apple. They knew then that they were no longer in London. They didn't know what to do. They knew they couldn't stay there, even though there were storybook characters everywhere! They wished to be back home, and suddenly that was exactly where they were! They realised what had happened at that moment; they had wished to be *inside* the book!

Sylvia Sinclair (11)
The Kingsley School For Girls, Leamington Spa

My Wonder

I was in a land that I did not know. It was bright everywhere; I mean *really* bright everywhere! It was amazing, but then again I was still completely clueless where I was. I had not had a good day. I had already been given detention from a teacher, and when I finally got home my mum shouted at me. I was sent up to my room. I noticed a strange book that I hadn't seen before. I opened it and it transported me to a strange world, seemingly in the middle of nowhere! Suddenly, a dark shadow passed me...

Izzie Gore (12)
The Kingsley School For Girls, Leamington Spa

In-Between Worlds

It was 2116 and the sun gleamed in through Caroline's window. She had made her choice and wanted to become a vampire. She had fallen in love with one and was ready to be with him forever. Her parents disapproved and everyone in the town hated vampires! Even her boyfriend thought it was a bad idea because he didn't want to put her in danger. She had made her choice however, and became a vampire! She could never see her parents again, but she sometimes saw them going about their business, somewhat sad that their daughter was gone.

Chantal Soiné (14)
The Kingsley School For Girls, Leamington Spa

Welcome To Wonderland

In the constellation of Kalabraxsos, in the year 3033, there was a human; the last of her kind. She looked happy and sad at the same time. She had travelled far; further than anything in existence. Too far to go back. She had gone into space to help out on the space station, but there was a solar flare. She survived, but the Earth was destroyed. She floated through space until she reached Kalabraxsos. The beings there accepted her as one of their own. She had an amazing life, until she found out that the flare had made her immortal...

Amber Venn

The Kingsley School For Girls, Leamington Spa

The Underground

The floorboards started to creak, and one of her new golden ballet pumps slipped off. As she completed her last pirouette, the floor fell in and she was no longer in the theatre. She fell and let out an ear-piercing scream. Madam Muzzel ran on stage and tried to grab her hand, but it was too late! Falling deeper and deeper, Anna reached what felt like solid ground. She was sat in a dark pit and suddenly she saw red, demonic eyes and a thin, bony hand creeping towards her. She screamed again. It was her last scream.

Matilda Milner (12)
The Kingsley School For Girls, Leamington Spa

The Light At The End

Windswept hair and with a beaten face, Maya still had one more challenge ahead of her; getting back. She was trapped under a blanket of snow from the avalanche she had just survived. She was determined to get home to her family and she burst out of the snow pile, using all her strength. She staggered along the path, weak and tired, but not ready to give up. She walked for miles and miles. She tried her best to ignore the blue light she saw on her way back, knowing she would die if she gave in to it...

Laura Jane Silk (13)
The Kingsley School For Girls, Leamington Spa

Alice In Reality

The darkness I woke up to was unlike anything I had ever seen before. Was I in a hole? I emerged from the hole, and saw... normality. The rabbits did not wear waistcoats and the people appeared painfully ordinary. I didn't understand what had happened or where I was. The whole world was gloomier than Wonderland and I hated it! Suddenly, I saw a familiar flash of white near a tree. I ran over there. It was the white rabbit! He told me he had been looking for me everywhere, and that it was time to return home!

Katie Jones (13)
The Kingsley School For Girls, Leamington Spa

The Lost Island

There was once a girl and she lived with her family. The girl was named Penelope, and her dream was going on a boat in the Pacific Ocean. After weeks of persuading her parents, they finally took her to the Pacific Ocean. On the boat, Penelope was looking at the fish pass by, when her big brother Philip pushed her in! The boat kept going and she was stranded there! She swam to the nearby island and waited there for someone to rescue her! She befriended a fairy there, and it helped get her parents' attention!

Phoebe Turner (11)
The Kingsley School For Girls, Leamington Spa

It's A Hard Life Being An Ant

I stopped in my tracks. A huge behemoth of a creature was standing in my way. I had heard about them on the news but I never believed they could exist! The media made them seem violent, but this one just stood there! Suddenly, it kneeled down and appeared to beckon me over. I climbed onto its hand and it stood again, starting to walk. I was high up. Extremely high up. Suddenly, it turned and looked at me. It used its other hand to flick me off! I went absolutely flying! It's a hard life being an ant...

Katie Walsh (14)

The Kingsley School For Girls, Leamington Spa

Welcome To Wonderland

Once, there was a girl named Willow. She was a mermaid who had beautiful curly ginger hair. She lived with her mother, Sienna. She had lovely rainbow scales just like her daughter. They lived in a little village right at the bottom of the ocean, called Merdale. One day, she and her mum saw a mysterious creature lingering on top of the water where the evil king mermaid lived. Sienna shouted at it to get away before the king mermaid killed it. The massive whale obliged and swam away to safety!

Ishika Doug (11)
The Kingsley School For Girls, Leamington Spa

Cloud World

The moment I set foot on the world, I realised it was different. The city nearby was a glistening white. I appeared to be in a city in the clouds! The people went bustling by, walking on nothing but the clouds. I learned that an evil man, Cloudman, was plotting to overthrow the queen! I agreed to help and I went to confront him. It turned out that the people in the city didn't accept him, and that was why he had turned to evil. I helped him get on their good side and soon everybody was happy!

Lily Lawson (13)
The Kingsley School For Girls, Leamington Spa

WELCOME TO WONDERLAND - WESTERN ENGLAND

Never Ever Land

Society can slap you in the face or it can give you a helping hand. There is one thing that society has never given anyone. Freedom. Genuine, unrestricted freedom.
One day, I was looking out of the window and I noticed that there was something flying towards me. A man! He tumbled into my room. He looked about my age. He told me that I could escape the confines of society if I went with him to Never Ever Land. I had nothing to lose and went with him to a land of opportunity and understanding!

Beth Rickett (13)
The Kingsley School For Girls, Leamington Spa

Horror And Humour

I woke up, as if I had been asleep for 100 years. As I opened my eyes, I saw something. It was a brightly-coloured funfair, with flashing lights and children running with fluffy candyfloss. However, on the other side there was a dark piece of land that continued for miles. It looked like a battlefield. I felt uneasy and went to ask one of the townsfolk for help. They told me how I could get home. I followed their instructions precisely. I teleported back home and woke up in my bed!

Abi Lawson (11)
The Kingsley School For Girls, Leamington Spa

Guardians

There was once a land named Orindale. Orindale was home to many people, such as: princes, princesses, goblins and witches.

On Earth, Lucy was having a nice walk by a cliff, when suddenly the cliff started to collapse and Lucy fell down into the darkest, blackest hole she had seen. She was falling. Below her was a light, brighter than bright. She opened her eyes, and she was in Orindale; a place that she had only read about in books! She became a princess there and lived a happy life!

Grace Green (12)
The Kingsley School For Girls, Leamington Spa

The Secret!

The condensation obscured the window pane, but as I peered outside I could just about see the first snowflake falling from the bleak sky above. Christmas had surely arrived! I felt a sudden rush of excitement. I was so captivated, I nearly missed the beep of my phone. I had a text from my friend Molly, saying she had a surprise. Wanting to find out what it was, I put on my coat and went to the park to meet her. She was standing there and at her feet was a fluorescent, smouldering object!

Isabella Larucci
The Kingsley School For Girls, Leamington Spa

Welcome To Wonderland

Miranda was coming home from school. It was very foggy. She wanted to go sit down on a bench but all the benches were full, except one that just had an annoying boy from her class on, named Jamie. She went to sit down anyway because her legs hurt so badly. They sat in dead silence. Suddenly, a train came into the station. The cold wind blew as the train left again, and they noticed a tree with a carving on it. It was Miranda's mum's and Jamie's dad's initials in a love heart!

Kitty Lawson (11)

The Kingsley School For Girls, Leamington Spa

Into The Unknown

I was looking at the murky forest which stood before me. It was the only way to get to the far side of the island, and I knew what I had to do. I stepped forward. The infested swamp was my first challenge. It was almost certain death to even attempt to cross. I had to cross the bridge to the other side. I carefully took step after step, but noticed that the bridge was creaking. Suddenly, the rope snapped and I fell in! I frantically tried to swim, but felt the sea dragons pulling me under...

Grace Heather Shipley (14)
The Kingsley School For Girls, Leamington Spa

White Cloth!

Beams of light flickered through the open window, catching the light of the glossy snow globe that had been placed on the mahogany table long ago. Only once had Cecilia ever seen the pure orb of frozen land. In her dreams she visualised stepping outside into the snow. One night, she saw a shimmering light and followed it. It led her to a magical snowy world! She realised she was in the snow globe! Suddenly, the whole world started shaking and snow was falling! Someone was shaking the globe!

Olivia Marshall (11)
The Kingsley School For Girls, Leamington Spa

The Lost Desert

Sanuta and Saffron were best friends. One day, they woke up in a desert! There was a sign in front of them, telling them that they were in the Sahara! They turned around and looked at the barren landscape; soft, orange sand beneath their feet. Suddenly, over the horizon, men in uniforms appeared holding machine guns and riding horses. They ran for their lives until they couldn't run any more. They turned around. They had lost them. They had no idea why the men were after them!

Amy Barrett (11)
The Kingsley School For Girls, Leamington Spa

The Push

It was a cold, dark afternoon. I went into the big city for the first time in four years. I stepped out of my house, holding my anxiety back as my mother had instructed, and got the bus into the city. I walked the streets, looking around at all the sights. Suddenly, all the people disappeared and the sky got dark. I felt a rush of fear throughout my body and collapsed onto my knees. I felt a cold hand grab my shoulder and I turned around to see a pair of demonic, red, glowing eyes!

Jessica Bennett
The Kingsley School For Girls, Leamington Spa

Lemuria

I was hungry, tired and needing a rest. I carried on running, however. The wind was blowing the hair out of my face. The day was almost over and I knew I would have to be back soon. I realised that I had run so far, I didn't know where I was! It was some sort of forest! I tripped and fell, blacking out. I awoke and found that I was surrounded by some hooded figures! They helped me up and welcomed me to their underground city of Lemuria; the last refuge of the Lemurhumans.

Georgie Green (14)
The Kingsley School For Girls, Leamington Spa

The Christmas Extravaganza!

I imagined a world. A world full of little elves dressed in their green uniforms. A world which smelled like a fire burning on a chilly winter night. It was Christmas World! There was crisp, white snow like the inside of a bounty bar and huge, musty, green Christmas trees raging above me in the shape of rockets. Suddenly, I spotted Santa! In his red suit, he looked a bit like the inside of a red velvet cake. I opened my eyes, and to my surprise I was there!

Charlotte Lucy Green (11)
The Kingsley School For Girls, Leamington Spa

Welcome To Wonderland

Max was an explorer and he saw a door built into a tree one day. He opened it and walked through. He ended up in a snowy Christmas village. It was beautiful. There was snow and there were so many bright lights! He was amazed. Suddenly, he turned around and saw some demonic snowmen! He ran for his life. He hid in a house, but they started breaking in! He didn't know what to do, so he wished to be back home.
Poof!
Suddenly, he was back in his bed!

Mia Featherstone (11)
The Kingsley School For Girls, Leamington Spa

The Deep Blue Ocean

Tara, a teenage girl, hated life. One day, she had had enough and decided to run away from home. She was running when, suddenly, a bright light enveloped her. She gasped in wonder as she was transported to the bottom of the ocean! She found that she could breathe! She saw some mermaids and they greeted her with open arms. She was very happy, happier than she had been in a long time. She decided to stay in Atlantis with the mermaids and she had a great life!

Sophie Elizabeth Maguire (13)
The Kingsley School For Girls, Leamington Spa

The Candy Can

I was running in the woods when I fell over a tree stump. I was unconscious for about thirty minutes. I woke up with a rabbit on my head. It was saying something about something that I had to eat to get back home. It told me to eat the grass and I did so. It immediately took me back home and I was relieved. I wondered about the rabbit and what had happened. I looked out of my window and saw the same rabbit, hopping into some bushes...

Morgan Anne Marie Bethell (12)
The Kingsley School For Girls, Leamington Spa

Bang!

Bang!
It's funny how similar shooting a gun is to taking a photo. You pick a target, point and *click*. A flash comes out. He fell like a ragdoll, down and down. The sea exploded around him and then he was gone. The sea had swallowed my secret. All that was left was the haunting howl and crash of the waves, attacking the black rocks below. It was over. I was free, but would I be able to outrun my conscience?

Pia Brougham (13)
The Kingsley School For Girls, Leamington Spa

Good Fortune...

There was once a baby born on the poor streets of India. His family were living in poverty, until one day they were approached by the rich king. The king didn't like to see people suffer, but couldn't step down because someone evil would take his place. He offered them money and a feast at his castle. They were extremely grateful and were able to live their lives without struggling, all thanks to the kind old king!

Maddie Mia McClean (13)

The Kingsley School For Girls, Leamington Spa

136

Who?

I was out walking and I suddenly saw a familiar man. I wasn't sure where I had seen him before. He had wispy, brown hair and his face was freckled. Just like mine. I stared at him and noticed that he was exactly the same as me! I got scared and ran home. When I got there, I saw him again! I began to realise that he only moved when I did... I asked my mum and she told me that it was called a reflection!

Grace Smith (14)
The Kingsley School For Girls, Leamington Spa

Welcome To Wonderland

I woke up earlier than usual one morning as I could finally go to Exorcists' school. My mum was really upset that I was leaving for school, but she was also extremely excited. She used to go to the school too, and she was one of the best exorcists there! I walked into the school, and immediately made friends. I got very good at performing exorcisms and I was soon top of every class! My mum was extremely proud of me!

Maya Illingworth (11)
The Kingsley School For Girls, Leamington Spa

WELCOME TO WONDERLAND - WESTERN ENGLAND

Welcome To Wonderland

I lived high in the clouds, where we watched the humans below. I was a child on Earth once. I lost my first tooth. I was sleeping upstairs and I heard a noise. I woke up and saw something with a golden glow squeeze through the key hole. It was a fairy! I fell back asleep suddenly. When I awoke again, I was surrounded by loads of fairies, and I noticed that I had wings too! I had become a fairy.

Eliza Chamberlain-Sparks (11)
The Kingsley School For Girls, Leamington Spa

Stone Heart's Tomb

One of the most famous treasure hunters, James Gardlen, was lurking near the so-called 'cursed' tomb of Stone Heart, the pirate. Sneaking around in the fog of demise, Gardlen finally saw it, the secret vault of Stone Heart. People say it can only be opened by using Stone Heart's handcrafted steel hook but Gardlen had a skeleton key which could open any door. It opened.

'Works like a charm,' he whispered smugly to himself.

He carelessly strolled to the prized possession of Stone Heart, his sapphire femur. Gardlen picked it.

'No!'

Spiked through the heart, his final resting place...

Will James Coadey (13)
Tuition, Medical & Behaviour Support Service, Bridgnorth

The Hundred Ways

As I drifted between consciousness, I glared deeply into the past: my daughter growing up without a father. I took a deep breath and descended into history.

'You did it!' exclaimed a voice close to my ear. 'You found the new world. It took us sixty years but we finally traced your beacon.'

'What do you mean sixty years?' I asked.

'Your life support kept you alive. We traced you through the beacon.'

'The last thing I remember was jumping towards my daughter... what happened?'

I turned slowly to my left and saw my daughter sleeping silently like an angel.

Leo Kane (14)
Tuition, Medical & Behaviour Support Service, Bridgnorth

Night Of The Hunter

The stench of blood perfumed the dark night air as Garret silently crept along the narrow street. He quickly glanced behind him to make sure he wasn't being followed. Satisfied that he was at last alone, he stepped out into the street. Pools of blood lay where the mangled corpses of people and beasts that had been slaughtered by hunters the night before.

Ravenous crows picked excitedly at the bodies, blood-soaked beaks diving in and out of the rotten carcasses. Garret unlocked the heavy iron door and stepped inside the only refuge in all of Mavengold, The Hunters' Hideaway.

Elliot Jones (14)
Tuition, Medical & Behaviour Support Service, Bridgnorth

Am I Home?

Falling. I was falling. The swirling tunnel twisted my vision like a vicious brain teaser. I didn't know when it would end. Everything was dark.

I woke up. I was in my bed, safe. Or so I thought. I walked out of my room and realised that my house had been destroyed! My bedroom was the only room left standing and the area surrounding it was just rubble! I couldn't see anyone... Suddenly, I spotted a figure on the hill. I shouted, thinking it was my family member. It headed towards me. I realised that it wasn't human at all...

Emily Cross (14)
West Midlands Construction UTC, Wolverhampton

Trapped

Cautiously sitting up, I turned around. The unfamiliar place was extremely gloomy, yet I managed to work out that it had four walls. They appeared to be closing in on me! I didn't know if I was going crazy but that was what I saw! Sure enough, as I tried to stagger forwards to find a door, I heard the rumbling as they moved even faster towards me. I used my brain and jumped up, grabbing hold of a metal grate. I hoisted myself up to safety as the walls closed. I heard a voice.
'Congratulations. Test passed.'

Georgina Tranter-Wilkes (15)
West Midlands Construction UTC, Wolverhampton

Borderland

I darted in-between the buildings, trying to dodge the Regime's relentless bullets. The air was infested with the smell of death and I had grown accustomed to it. Shattered windows looked down at me. Fractured pavements slithered down the road like serpents; cradling the buildings and suffocating them to the point of collapse. Hearing a vehicle's engine, I panicked and dived into a nearby building. I was the last human alive on Earth and I needed to survive...

Gurpal Singh Sahota (14)
West Midlands Construction UTC, Wolverhampton

Vampire Academy

I warned the princess to stay close and keep her wits about her. We walked through the streets of Los Angeles, looking for any sign of someone who would want to harm her. She had received a death threat a few days before from an anonymous person, and as her protector, it was my job to defend her. She was the last of her bloodline. She was a vampire, and we were bonded by friendship. I successfully guided her to the safe house and we stayed there for the night!

Danielle Lace Bowdler-Silvester (15)

West Midlands Construction UTC, Wolverhampton

Nobody

Surprised they're not here yet. Could be the traffic I suppose. It can be a nightmare this time of the morning. Wonder if I've time for another coffee? What shall I tell them when they arrive? Maybe turn on the tears, say it was all a horrible mistake? I didn't mean to do it. He attacked me first. That sort of thing. Not true of course. I know exactly what is going to happen. Surely they've found his body by now; why aren't they here?

Jai Ghai (14)
West Midlands Construction UTC, Wolverhampton

The Man Behind The Mask

Shot dead! No second thought was given when the trigger was pulled. My thighs began to shake and I couldn't feel my hands. Taking a quick glance at the bloody body laying in front of me, I felt a pang of sadness. My eyes turned to the man who had shot her. I saw my own eyes glaring back. It was a mirror...

I knew that what I had done was necessary for the survival of the human race, but she was still innocent and didn't deserve to die.

Gurkeitan Singh Barring (14)
West Midlands Construction UTC, Wolverhampton

YoungWriters
Est.1991

YOUNG WRITERS INFORMATION

We hope you have enjoyed reading this book – and that you will continue to in the coming years.

If you're a young writer who enjoys reading and creative writing, or the parent of an enthusiastic poet or story writer, do visit our website **www.youngwriters.co.uk**. Here you will find free competitions, workshops and games, as well as recommended reads, a poetry glossary and our blog.

If you would like to order further copies of this book, or any of our other titles, then please give us a call or visit **www.youngwriters.co.uk**.

Young Writers
Remus House
Coltsfoot Drive
Peterborough
PE2 9BF
(01733) 890066
info@youngwriters.co.uk